About the author

Dr Gerloch retired in 1999 from a career as an academic and research scientist in the field of quantum chemistry in the University of Cambridge. He is an emeritus fellow of Trinity Hall. He and his wife, Gwyneth, have since lived in Canberra, Australia. During his first twenty years of blissful retired domesticity, Malcolm has enjoyed gardening, house renovation and above all, learning to cook in several cuisines. Gwyneth has relinquished the kitchen with mixed feelings. Prior to writing children's books, Malcolm's greatest achievement has been the construction of a dual-manual harpsichord for his wife to play. That was a present to thank her for introducing him to the non-scientific literature of — mostly — the nineteenth and twentieth century European and twentieth century North American writers.

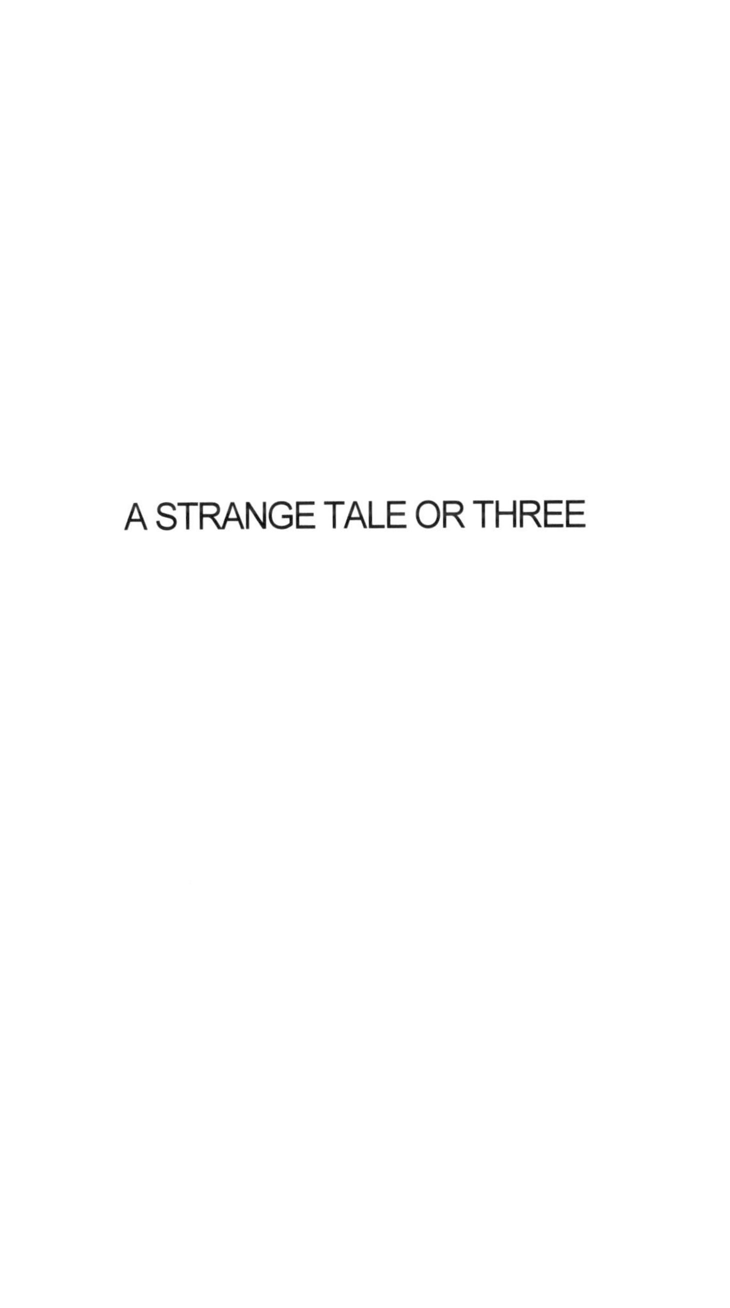

A STRANGE TALE OR THREE

Malcolm Gerloch

A STRANGE TALE OR THREE

Vanguard Press

VANGUARD PAPERBACK

© Copyright 2021
Malcolm Gerloch

The right of Malcolm Gerloch to be identified as author of
this work has been asserted by him in accordance with the
Copyright, Designs and Patents Act 1988.

A CIP catalogue record for this title is
available from the British Library.

ISBN 978 1 80016 239 6

*Vanguard Press is an imprint of
Pegasus Elliot MacKenzie Publishers Ltd.*
www.pegasuspublishers.com

First Published in 2021

**Vanguard Press
Sheraton House Castle Park
Cambridge England**

Printed & Bound in Great Britain

*Other books for younger readers
by Malcolm Gerloch*

Bird
Bahs
Flea
Spike

Rosie 'N' Co.
Zada

and by Malcolm Gerloch and Gwyneth Gerloch

Chook

and for adult readers by Malcolm Gerloch

Old Harald and Other Stories

Dedication

In everlasting gratitude to everyone who has taught me, in school and out, both formally and informally.

Acknowledgements

As ever, my wife, Gwyneth has read my stuff so often and offered so many suggestions along the way that I simply had to accept some of them. Her love has sustained me more than I can ever say.

Contents

BUTTON

Playback begins:

I had an hour-or-so's journey ahead of me but that was fine. It was a nice sunny day and I was driving through some pleasant countryside to spend time with Glen, an old friend whom I had known for many years. He had invited a small group of his friends for a buffet lunch and a catch-up. I'd not been to his new home before so everything along the route was new and interesting to me. In amongst many quite ordinary, trees I spotted several clumps of palm. It really seemed odd to see them there for I was certainly not driving in the tropics. Still, palm trees do grow in more temperate areas, though not often.

I had been driving through some rolling country for quite a while but by the time that my satnav was telling me that I was only five minutes away from his place on the edge of a small village called Cottwell, the land was nearly flat. I think that's right. I slowed down near Glen's house and turned into a short level driveway and parked the car next to a large clump of two-metre-high black bamboo.

There was a winding gravel path up to his front door, which was framed, as it were, by several palm trees on either side. As if that weren't grand enough, the door itself turned out to be something rather memorable. The house overall was nice enough but quite unexceptional, I would say, but that front door seemed so important. It was made up of some quite beautiful raised and fielded oak panels and there was a large and splendid brass knob in the middle. On either side of this magnificent mahogany door were bevelled glass panels through which I could see several leafy plants inside an impressive hallway. I suppose my attention was so drawn to all this because it seemed so different from anything Glen had lived in before. It was not out of place with the rest of the house, however, which turned out to be an architectural gem. I didn't remember Glen being rich enough to own a house as grand as this but assumed that he'd come into money somehow. None of my business! Glen wouldn't have chosen a pine front door like that, I felt. Goodness, it's only a front door; why get so hung up about it?

Inside, a couple of Glen's other friends had already arrived and were chatting and laughing together. I knew both of them and joined in with their talk. But then I suddenly remembered that I'd had a small problem with my car door on the journey and mentioned this to Glen, who surprised me by saying that he had a mechanic in his garage at the bottom of the garden who could fix it for me. I thought it odd for anyone to have a mechanic on tap, but I accepted Glen's offer nevertheless.

Lunch appeared after a while and we all sat down at a table laid for twelve to a delightful four-course affair which went on for several hours. I made several new friends around that table and declared to one and all how pleasant my day had turned out.

Much of our conversation was about sharing memories. Do you remember where we first met? Was that a yellow car or green? Was it raining or sunny? At one point, talk got around to the idea of premonition and memory and about how they could get mixed up with each other. The point is that while memory is concerned with things past, premonition is about things future. So how do you know whether a thought, say a data stream like seeing an event or hearing a conversation (just like the data streams you'd get from Netflix, for example) is from the past or the future? Of course, there might be some images of clocks in your sensations but what if there weren't? How do you know whether you are experiencing a memory or a premonition?

'Yes, and worse,' said Roger, one of Glen's friends at table who I hadn't met before. 'You might be remembering a premonition!'

'Or anticipating a memory!' Rodney, another of the lunch guests, interjected.

'Or remembering anticipating a memory!' yelled Robin from the far end of the table.

'All that,' I laughed. 'It's rather like a hall of mirrors where you stand between two mirrors which face each other. As you turn to look at your reflection in one mirror, you can see the back of your head and then, further away, your face again and so on and so on. You see a reflection of a reflection of a reflection… seemingly forever.' This was all getting rather complicated and I began to wonder if I was really there at all.

It was at about half past four when I got up and said my goodbyes to one and all, thanked my host, and began to leave the house the way I had come in.

'Oh, don't go that way,' Glen said. 'Go out the back way so you can pick up your car from my garage.' As I left the house, I noticed how steeply the ground sloped away from the house down to Glen's garage at the bottom of the garden. I'd not noticed any hilly ground nearby before but maybe I'd been mistaken. As I approached the garage, I found that the road outside was completely flooded; indeed, there was a torrent of water rushing past. It wasn't raining though and, as far as I could recall, it hadn't rained while we had been inside at the buffet. I supposed that all that water must have come from some area much further away where it had rained. But so much water! It was rushing past so quickly that the road surface had been partly swept away and the river, as it now was, was rushing past huge mounds of mud. I looked further along the road and saw that the flood extended for some way but now covered a wider though shallower path. The sunny day I had experienced on my outward journey had now given way to a blustery, cold and cloudy one which was really depressing.

'How will I get my car out of the garage?' I wondered.

Actually, I must have said it out loud because a man I took to be Glen's mechanic came out of the garage and said, 'Don't worry! We saw what was happening some time ago and, since I'd finished your little repair, I moved the car away from the area and it's now on safe dry ground.'

I thanked him profusely and asked where he'd left it.

He pointed towards a tiny hamlet about a kilometre away and said, 'There, just on the side of the road; it's not far and you can get to it without wading through any water.'

I looked where he'd pointed and could see a few cars including the grey one I was looking for. I thanked him again and set off.

I'd been walking for some time before I got to those cars by the side of the road. There were four but none was mine. Then I noticed a small field just behind where they were parked and found that that field was itself a small car park. I hadn't noticed it before, which I found odd. Never mind, I began looking for my car in the car park. I couldn't see it at first and kept walking up and down the rows of vehicles. I noticed that there seemed to be many more cars in that park than I had originally thought. And the car park wasn't a field after all but was sealed and quite dry. It took quite a time to look all over for my car. It wasn't there. What I did see, though, was that the hamlet I'd seen in the distance from Glen's house was now only a few hundred metres beyond the car park. I don't know why exactly, but I thought I'd go to the village and have a look around.

Even before I arrived there, I could see that I'd stumbled across a sort of market being held beside some buildings on one side and yet another car park on the other. There appeared to be few people around. Immediately, of course, I began searching this new car park for my car, but without any luck. It was about then that I began to wonder if I had come to Glen's place that morning in a hire-car or a borrowed car because I was getting uncertain about what car I was looking for. Was it grey or blue? Was my car a Mercedes or a Toyota? This was getting silly. Of course, I'd recognise my car as soon as I saw it and then I'd be off. But I couldn't find any car I recognised in the very large, car park. I thought it might be a good idea to see if I could find someone to ask in the buildings beside the market.

Those buildings turned out to be rather larger and more extensive than I'd first thought. There were two rows of shops separated by a small paved area where people were rushing back and forth all over the place like the busy shoppers they were. I didn't know who to speak to or, for that matter, quite what to ask, so I walked along the paved street heading in roughly the same direction I had originally taken after leaving Glen's house. As I got near the end of this paved street, I saw yet another car park outside and beyond the village. Maybe Glen's mechanic had meant that he'd parked the car here? Off I went looking again and, once more, I found no sign of a green Ford anywhere. I just knew I'd know it as soon as I saw it. But I didn't see it. In some confusion, I turned back into the town buildings. I found that the paved street was actually part of a shopping mall. I saw a café and decided to pop in for a coffee while I thought things over.

I found a small unoccupied table and sat down. A waitress came and I ordered a flat white coffee. It was while I was waiting for it to arrive, that a man came to my table and asked if he might sit at my table for there were no other vacant places.

'That's fine.' I said, 'Do please join me.' I couldn't help staring at this bloke for I felt sure that I knew him from somewhere. Then I realised. Much older now — but then, so was I — he was our old maths teacher from schooldays.

'You're Roger!' I said with some excitement, 'Roger, er… sorry I've just forgotten your surname. You taught maths at Burlingham High.'

'That's right,' he replied, 'but forgive me, I don't remember you, I'm afraid.'

I excitedly explained who I was, when I had been at the school, and which class he had taught me in.

Then he remembered. 'Gosh, that was a long time ago!' he said. And it was, of course.

I reminded Roger of the day he lost his whole class. 'It wasn't my class,' I explained, 'but the story was all round the school.'

'Oh yes, I remember that,' he laughed. 'I was very inexperienced in those early days of my career. I had turned my back to the class and was writing up the proof of Pythagoras' theorem on the chalkboard. Do you remember those old chalkboards, by the way? We would write on a large board painted with a matt black paint, using cylindrical sticks of chalk nearly ten centimetres long and about one-and-a-half in diameter. Afterwards, we would clean off what was written, or drawn, with a cloth or a board cleaner made of felt attached to a wooden handgrip. You usually got clouds of chalk dust all over you! Very messy! Actually, one of my colleagues at that school used the "wing" of his gown to clean the board. He had little respect for the idea of teachers wearing gowns, so he just used his as a duster.

'Anyway, there I was writing out Pythagoras' theorem. It's quite a difficult proof and takes some time to write up fully. I heard some scuffling behind me but didn't bother to turn around. I just said, "Be quiet and copy this proof into your notebooks". Everything went quiet for quite some time. Eventually, when I had finished writing out the proof, I turned around. The whole class of twenty-odd boys had disappeared. There wasn't a soul in the room. I was amazed. I opened the classroom door and went outside into the corridor to see if they were there but there was absolutely nobody around. I even walked down into the main school hall in search of my class. There was simply no sign of them. I returned to the classroom and sat down at my desk wondering what I should do. That was when I heard shuffling and a repressed giggle coming from the cupboards at the back of the room. The classroom we were in was normally used for geography lessons and it had enormous cupboards to house all sorts of map rolls, rock samples, models and that sort of thing. I walked to the back of the room and opened one of the cupboard doors, there to find the whole of my class in a heap. They thought it was hugely funny, of course. Unfortunately, so did my colleagues in the staff room when they got to hear about it, which took only minutes because those sorts of things get around a school in no time. I was quite a laughingstock and all the other teachers saw how green I was.'

'And then you went off to the US for a year on an exchange with an American teacher who spent the year with us in England,' I said. 'I remember his being rattled by the general attitude of English boys. It was while we were outside on the playing fields watching one of our rugby matches. He saw how serious most boys were about the game and he remarked, "I don't get it. Inside the school during your lessons, you never shut up. You're always making remarks and playing the fool. But outside at your sports, you are nearly silent and paying full attention to the game. It's just the opposite to what goes on back in the States".

'We were quite amused and suggested, "Well sir, so you've learned something from your time over here!" We were very cheeky, I suppose. Anyway, when you came back from the States, Roger, you were utterly different. Nobody would have dreamed about climbing into cupboards or any other foolery in your classes then. I remember the first lesson you gave my class after coming home. You walked into the classroom and said, "Good morning, gentlemen!" Nobody had ever called us gentlemen before. We were gobsmacked and simply replied, "Good morning, sir". From that moment onwards, no boy in any of the school's classes ever tried mucking about with you. We weren't scared of you or anything; we just wanted to do the right thing.'

'I know; I had learned a great deal during my year in the US and become rather confident,' Roger replied.

We had a good laugh but then I noticed that Roger's face had changed a bit. I couldn't say how but he seemed different and his voice seemed to come from further away. I felt a bit funny about it really but can't say how exactly. We talked about other things we remembered from the old days, although our memories didn't exactly agree all the time.

Oh well, I thought, *memory plays tricks sometimes.*

After a while, we left the café and I went for a walk around the shopping mall. Actually, it seemed to be a larger shopping mall than I remembered it when I came into the café, I thought, but I wasn't sure about that. I walked onto an escalator and went up to the next floor where I came across a shop selling all kinds of car parts. I thought how useful that would be to Glen's mechanic who had fixed my car and that reminded me that I was still looking for a car.

Trouble was that I now couldn't find the way out of the mall and the car park. I remembered that I'd begun on the ground floor but now I found an exit on the first floor. After a very short walk, really, I suddenly came across a pathway along which were several houses which looked like Glen's. At the end of a short row, I found one with his unique front door. Panelled sycamore with a gilded door ring on one side. I rushed up to that beautiful and, oh! so familiar, door and was about to knock when I began to realise that something wasn't quite right. The door wasn't exactly as I remembered it although it seemed amazing to me that there'd be another similar. And anyway, how could this be Glen's place because I had walked a long, long way from his house to get to this town so how could his house be right outside the mall? More puzzling still was that a face appeared at one of the house windows and that face was very similar to Glen's! I waved but it just stared back at me.

I decided to backtrack into the mall again. At least that was okay. The mall was still there but at the top of the escalator there was a small garden with black bamboo, some palm trees and a few seats beneath them. I sat down on one to collect my thoughts. I looked around and saw five possible directions in which to search. Search for what, though? Why was I there? What should I do next? I wasn't unduly worried, however, and was quite happy to go for a stroll, choosing one of the seven possible paths at random. I came across a small café and, fancying a coffee, wandered in and sat down at a small table and looked around. The place was pretty full, and I had to wait quite a while before a waiter came for my order. I picked up a newspaper which was lying around and began to scan it casually. I came across an article about someone's car being washed away in a flood somewhere. I must say, I was feeling rather sorry for that person and read on to see where all this had happened. I discovered that not too far away, a man had been trapped in his vehicle which was floating away. So far, the article said, he had not been rescued. It seems that he had been on his way to visit a friend nearby when he was caught in a freak storm.

My reading was interrupted by a man asking to share my table.

'I hope you don't mind,' he said, 'but there are no free seats anywhere else.'

I didn't mind and continued to read the story about the cat which was swept away in a flood nearby.

After a while, the stranger said, 'Excuse me, but haven't we met before somewhere?'

I didn't think so but was happy to talk anyway.

'Aren't you Robert — sorry, but I've forgotten your surname; we were students at Burtigan High School many years ago.'

'Yes, I was there,' I replied, 'but I'm afraid I don't remember you. It has been a long time after all.'

'Oh, that's all right. I sometimes come across people I think I don't know but after talking with them for a while, I gradually realise that I do.'

We talked about the school for a bit before I said, 'It's funny our meeting up like this, Roger, because I think the last time we met, was in a cupboard at the back of the geography room where we and the rest of the class were hiding from the maths teacher. What was his name? I've forgotten.'

'Me too,' Roger laughed, 'but I do remember that business in the cupboards. Everyone in the school got to hear about it in minutes. The place was ringing with laughter at the prank we had pulled.'

'It's funny what things you remember about your school days,' I said. 'Do you remember Peter Jones in 4C who used to wear a monocle around the school? All for effect, of course.'

'Oh yes; but actually, he was quite bright as I recall and was in 4A rather than 4C.' He was probably right; I was getting muddled. 'The form master was a bloke called Anthony Bower,' he continued. 'He was an awfully nice man who tried to teach us Latin. Most of us were useless at that subject and we would play him up all the time. Like that maths teacher, Anthony had a habit of turning his back on his class while he wrote stuff up on the board. He liked to do that neatly, so he wrote slowly and took his time. So much time, in fact, that once, we students all shuffled our desks forward slowly and as quietly as possible so that, by the time Anthony had finished at the board and turned around, he found himself hemmed in by a circle of desks close up to him. We all pretended that nothing had happened. And so did he! He finished the lesson without saying a word about our "march".'

'Yes, I remember that,' I cried in delight, 'but, at the end of the lesson when the bell rang and as we were all getting up to go to our next class, Anthony said, quite quietly, "Put the desks back before you leave". We had assumed that he hadn't seen what we'd done. How stupid we were! Anthony Bowler had a fine sense of humour, really, and I guess he really liked school kids despite — or maybe because — of our pranks.'

'Do you remember what Chris Reynolds used to do with Anthony's gown? Rodney asked.

'Remind me,' I said, because I didn't.

'Well, all the masters would wear their MA gowns in class.'

'They don't do such a thing these days!' I laughed.

'I know, but those gowns had a sort of bag or wing part of the sleeve which hung down below the elbow. Anthony would stand between two of the front-row desks — it was always the same two desks, I remember

— and rock back and forth on his heels while he was spouting Latin at us.'

'Yes, yes, I remember now,' I enthused.

'Well, Chris Reynolds would drop bits of rubbish, like a crumpled piece of paper or a piece of chalk, into the sleeve bag of Anthony's gown without his knowing.'

'I remember that,' I said. It was all coming back very clearly. Ronald continued his story.

'The best bit, though, was that by the end of the term that bag got so much junk in it that, as Anthony swung his arms, the bag would swing strongly like a pendulum. Actually,' he laughed, 'Anthony began to list a bit.'

'Yes, I remember now,' I said, 'On the last day of term, Anthony quietly took Chris Remer aside, took off his gown and said, "Empty it out, Charles. Into the bin". For some reason, Anthony always called Chris, Charles. He did have an odd sense of humour! Anyway, Chris emptied out the sleeve bag into the bin and you should have seen what had been in there. Not only paper and chalk but chewing gum and sweets, a razor blade, bits of bent wire, a coin or two, a screwed-up used toothpaste tube — you know, the sort that were made out of heavy tin or lead or something rather than of plastic, as they are today — a small empty medicine bottle and an artificial (thank heavens) dead mouse. No wonder the old boy had begun to list. And Anthony had obviously known about it all from the beginning. His joke was just not to let on. Yes, I really do remember that teacher with a great deal of affection.'

Oh, we did so enjoy reminiscing about our school days.

'I wonder if girls remember the same sorts of things from their schooldays,' I mused.

'I'm not too sure about that,' Roger replied, 'My sister, Zoe, once told me that her memories of schoolgirl pranks were often about being mean or sneaky to each other although she did remember having fun with one of her science teachers. He had quickly made a model of the solar system by threading lumps of bread on loops of wire. The bread represented the various planets, with the sun in the middle, while the wires showed planetary paths around the sun. It wasn't a marvellous model but was quite good enough to get the teacher's points across. While his back was turned, a couple of the girls pinched one or two of the bread planets and ate them! They boasted afterwards that they had eaten Venus and Mars.'

'I guess girls are more interested in psychology and personality than are boys,' I said.

'I'm not sure. It might be about power. Anyway, my sister was very proud of how she could swear and curse when she was little — probably around eight or nine, I would guess. When she got very angry about something, but not too angry to lose control, she would perform a kind of act for her audience. Stamping her foot in time, she would call out as loudly as she could, "Bums, boobs, wee-wee, poo!" She sometimes does it even now as a grown-up. I think it's hilarious.'

I don't know how long Robin and I sat chatting but eventually we decided to get up and part company. I resumed my search. But what for? I walked back towards the escalators with those palm trees and then followed a narrower passage than the one I'd just been down. It seemed to go a long way without getting anywhere interesting and, as time went by, it began to curve ever more tightly. A bit like a snail's shell, I thought. Eventually, it came to a dead end with just one door to be seen.

The door was a rather splendid affair, rather like something I'd seen only recently; wooden — ebony, I think — and made up into large raised and fielded panels. There was a large wooden knob in the middle which I turned. The door opened easily, and I passed through into an area which was considerably wider than it was deep and on the long wall opposite, there were ten or so smaller doors, each being made in a similar style to the one I'd just passed through. I opened one at random and found dozens of people inside who all laughed as the door opened and fell out in a heap on the floor. Then they rushed out past me the way I had come. I didn't feel that they were laughing at me, though; rather that they were all just happy people, having a joke on the world.

I began to retrace my steps until — and I don't really know how it happened — I ended up in the multistory carpark outside the building. I knew that I was supposed to be looking for something, so I began walking past lines of shopping trolleys which were lined up in rows like soldiers. Everything was so neat. I looked very hard but couldn't find the basket I was looking for. I wasn't sure how I would recognise it when, or if, I saw it.

I climbed some stairs to the next level up and was amazed to see rows of trolleys floating in a fast-moving stream of water. I was being swept along myself and only found safety when the basket I was in got caught up in a dense thicket of black bamboo. I would have been much better off in a car, I thought. It was then that I remembered that I was supposed to be looking for a car; my car, maybe? I think it had been repaired and now had a panelled, wooden door on the driver's side. No, that couldn't be right. It was no good. I couldn't remember which car I was looking for or what make it was, not even the colour.

I thought I'd go back to Glen's place and ask the mechanic to take me to the car. I began walking away from the shopping centre and the town but I couldn't see where Glen's house was at all. I was beginning to panic but had the presence of mind to stop and ask a passer-by to help me. I began to explain my predicament but found that I could no longer get my words out properly. Some words were simply wrong. I knew that, but couldn't help myself. Other words came out silently; I mouthed them but there was no sound. Several words did sound but came out broken or fractured. It was like a picture dissolving before my eyes, before my ears. The person I had accosted was staring uneasily at me as my knees started to give way and I, quite slowly, sank onto the ground. It's an emergency, I thought, and I tried to tell the (by now) several people around me… something… button.

…playback ends.

There was a short report in that evening's newspaper:

Police were called to the local Codwell market carpark where there had been a disturbance. A man had "slowly collapsed", onlookers reported. "It was just after he had begun saying something," said Mr Jo Hicks (36). "I don't know what he was saying because it was so garbled. He didn't sound drunk though. It was more like a recording machine breaking down; or rather, breaking up. All I could catch was something about a button… that was it, a button. I called the police and ambulance straight away." Paramedics were unable to resuscitate the man, however, and he was transported to the local hospital mortuary.

In due course, when doctors were sure that the stranger was quite dead, an autopsy was ordered and the procedure began, as ever, with the removal of the stranger's clothes. The pathologist's assistant had unbuttoned his shirt at the front and was loosening his trouser belt. But there, he was amazed to see, instead of a normal navel, a red, plastic button about two centimetres in diameter.

'Look at this,' he cried out to his boss.

'Ah,' she said, 'I've only once before seen one of those.' And she had been a pathologist for some twenty-five years. 'See if there's anything written on the button,' she continued.

Her assistant looked carefully and made out the word "Emergency". Without thinking about it, he pressed the red button. Ten seconds later, a mobile phone which lay in a pile of the stranger's possessions on a bench at the side, rang. Startled, the pathologist's assistant picked up the phone, accepted the call, and heard a voice tell him, 'Do nothing at all — absolutely nothing. We'll be with you within thirty minutes. Everything is okay. Don't worry.' The caller hung up.

'What the…' the startled assistant cried.

'Now the fun begins,' his boss said. 'You wait, there'll be a couple of wiz-kids here in a trice, complete with their boxes of tricks. I'll bet our patient is called "Robert" and, for sure, he ain't dead. Or maybe, he was never alive!'

Playback resumes:

I remember being picked up and having something put on my back for a while. And then…

'Hey! I got lost,' I told the engineer, 'and I couldn't find my car. I must get back to Glen's place. I'll take a cab.'

All was well. I felt fine and was beginning to sift through some silly memories. I knew that all would be clear after a few minutes. It often happens that way with robots like us. We must get that dropping-out business sorted however. It's not really dangerous but it is embarrassing.

...end.

YOU

Mirror, Mirror, on the Wall…

It all began for Peter when he decided to pay another visit to that junk shop in the main street. He wasn't looking for anything in particular. He just felt like browsing. He'd always enjoyed rummaging through piles of odd-looking stuff. Stuff which most people didn't want but, as Raymond, the shop owner, always said, there's always someone, somewhere… He'd once found a special sort of screwdriver which went around corners. On another occasion, he'd bought a joke book with half of a magician's handbook. It seemed that the joke was that the answers to the magician's problems were missing. He was working on it. Even earlier, he had found a set of skeleton keys. He bought them more for the ring on which they were kept. Peter liked the skull motif inlaid into the metal. None of these things was expensive, for Peter had little money, but they were all important in some way to him.

On this rather dank Tuesday afternoon in the first week of school holidays, there was nothing obvious to catch his eye. That often happened. But then he saw it. It was half-hidden behind the old shopkeeper's coat hanging on a hook behind the door. A statue. Well, a bust really, about forty centimetres high, carved out of some sort of sandstone. The head wasn't particularly distinguished; it wasn't particularly anything, actually. But there was something about the empty expression in the eyes together with a rather noble bearing in the angle and tilt of the head that appealed to Peter. He looked away but just couldn't resist looking back at it again; and again. Curiously, the bust was behind glass and contained within a substantial wooden frame so that, at first glance, the whole thing seemed more like a portrait than a statue.

'Who was the sculptor?' Peter asked the shop owner.

'It's by a lady I only know as Mrs Heatherington. All I've heard about her is that she lives in Linghelm Place, not too far from here,' he replied. 'I believe she carves quite a few heads and things.'

Peter looked again at the head behind the glass and felt overwhelmed by a compulsion to have it. It wasn't like the time he had bought the bent screwdriver or the joke book. He just kind of liked those things but this time he knew that he simply *must* have this bust. The frame was a bit scratched which was probably why the whole thing was priced at only one pound.

'I'll give you half a quid for it,' said Peter, trying it on with the old boy. The man must have been a bit tired that day because he didn't argue; Peter was a bit disappointed not to have enjoyed a wrangle with him for the old boy simply agreed.

'Done!' was all he said and that was that.

Peter took his bargain home and straight up to his own room. He found a suitable place for his statue on top of a tall chest of drawers. He placed the bust with its face almost exactly opposite Peter's own.

'Well, Statue,' Peter said to it — and he never got around to giving it any other name — 'welcome to your new home. I hope you will be very happy here.'

The statue stared blankly back at Peter. It was all one could expect. Peter had placed the statue in that position more by compulsion than from any sense of symmetry or decorative sensibility. It just had to be there, where he'd see it face to face, so to speak, every time he walked anywhere near it. He'd known the correct spot from the moment he got it home; maybe he'd known it even before that. The thing was that seeing Statue looking straight at him whenever he turned his gaze in that direction felt to Peter as if he were looking into a mirror. The frame and glazing in front of the bust were probably responsible for that. He tried pulling faces at Statue as if he were indeed looking in a mirror. After a while, he could almost swear that the statue smiled back at him. Only a very slight smile; a minute curve at one end of its mouth; the suggestion of a crease at the outer terminus of one eye. That made Peter smile himself. The idea of a piece of stone changing its expression was ridiculous, of course, but he liked the thought.

He liked the idea even more when, the next day, he said, half to himself and half to the statue, that he'd spend the money he'd saved by getting his new acquisition so cheaply on a bunch of flowers for his mum. He was certain Statue had smiled at that. There was surely just a little smile, wasn't there? Well anyway, off went Peter to the florist on the corner and returned with a nice posy for Mum who was ever so pleased and just a little surprised. She thanked Peter for his thoughtfulness but asked him to consider helping out their neighbour, Mrs Morris. Apparently, Mrs Morris had tripped and fallen down a couple of stairs, twisting her ankle in the process. Her doctor had bound it up and given her instructions to keep off it as far as possible for a week. So, she was temporarily housebound and couldn't do her weekly shop.

'How about your popping round and offering to do her shopping for her?' asked Peter's mum.

It was a simple enough request, but Peter was not keen on Mrs Morris. When he was much younger (all of two years), he had been in the habit of kicking a ball around in his back garden and rather too often, it would end up in Mrs Morris's garden. After the first couple of times this had happened, she had become rather angry and complained to Peter's mother, saying:

'One more time, and I'll keep the ball and sell it for charity.'

So, Peter made a face when his mum suggested he help out their neighbour.

'Think about it, Peter,' his mum had said, and he went up to his room to do just that.

'I know it would be a good thing to help her out,' he said to Statue, 'but she was mean to me over my playing football. Why should I do her shopping?'

Statue looked impassive. Peter picked up one of his computer magazines and flipped through a few pages. After a while, he continued his conversation:

'I mean, after all, I did apologise for the football at the time, so this isn't like making up after all this time, is it?'

Statue looked impassive. Sort of, thought Peter, but maybe there's a frown; a slight downturn of the mouth and its eyes seem to be a little narrower.

This is nuts, he thought. *It's almost as if Statue is disapproving. Oh, all right*, he thought, *I'll do the old biddy's shopping for her*, and sauntered downstairs.

'I'm going next door,' he shouted to his mum and went outside and round to Mrs Morris's house.

He got no answer to his knocking and then realised that, if she was confined to a chair or something, she wouldn't be able to come to the door. He tried turning the doorknob, the door opened, and he heard Mrs Morris's voice calling, 'Come in.'

Peter explained why he was there. Mrs Morris was really surprised and so grateful. She told him to sit down for a little while until she finished off her shopping list and then handed it to Peter with her purse.

'I think there should be enough money there,' she told him. 'You should be able to get everything at the supermarket in Dean Street.'

It took him about an hour and a half altogether — maybe a bit more, he wasn't sure — before he returned with several large bags filled with groceries of various kinds. Mrs Morris just beamed at him as he came in. She was so pleased,

'So grateful,' she said. 'That was extremely kind of you.'

Peter gave back her purse. She opened it and took out a note to give to him. For a second, he was tempted, but declined, saying, 'No, thank you very much, Mrs Morris, there is no need for that. I'm just glad I could help you.' And he left.

His mother greeted him when he got in and she too told him how pleased she was at what he'd done.

When he got to his room, he told Statue. This time, he was sure he could see the mouth twitch and the eyes widen. Ever so little but he was sure that Statue had approved. He thought he saw Statue's mouth move again, as if to say something. Its expression suddenly reminded him of something his friend, Mr Best, had told him several months ago.

Mr Best was a neighbour, living about eight houses along their street. He was nearly seventy years old, Peter had heard from his mum and dad. Mr and Mrs Best lived a very quiet life largely because, for years, Mr Best had suffered from a terrible problem with his sight. He had cataracts in both eyes, Mum had told Peter. Apparently, opaque skin had gradually grown over the lens — in each eye — so that all he could see was vague shadowy figures behind a white screen. These cataracts had grown quite slowly for many years so that Mr Best had known that blindness awaited him eventually. His father had suffered a similar problem and had undergone some surgery which had left him completely blind. At the age of sixty-nine, Mr Best himself, underwent surgery to remove his cataracts. He had been terrified that the same fate awaited him. But surgical skills had improved enormously since his father's day, and Mr Best's operation was completely successful. He had to wear "bottle-end" glasses, meaning spectacles with very strong lenses, but he could otherwise see perfectly well. He and his wife were so incredibly happy at the outcome that they began at last to interact with people at that rather late stage of their lives.

One day, in conversation with Mrs Best, Peter's mum heard that Mr Best played chess. Peter was mad keen on the game himself and went to see if Mr Best would give him a game occasionally. The old man was delighted, and there developed a regular meeting between the young Peter and the old Mr Best. (Peter knew his name was George but never called him that; to his face or even behind his back.) Mr Best was fifteen or more years older than Peter's dad, so it felt to Peter that he was visiting a grandfather. So it was, that every Wednesday evening, Peter would turn up at the Bests' at seven p.m. for an evening of chess. They would play quietly until about a quarter to nine, when Mrs Best would get up from her reading or knitting, as the case may be, to make a pot of tea which she invariably served with delicious home-made scones or biscuits. Over refreshments, Mr Best would ask Peter about his schoolwork. At first, Peter would reply very briefly for he was somewhat embarrassed by the questioning. But Mr Best insisted that Peter explain everything in minutest detail.

'How do I know you understand it if you cannot explain it to me?' he would say. Peter eventually became quite good at explaining things.

On one of these evenings with Mr Best, the subject got around to the question of responsibility for one's actions. Peter was trying to blame someone else at school for something he had done wrong himself. It wasn't an important thing, but Mr Best came out very strongly on the subject indeed. Without getting too heavy, Mr Best said that he believed that everything that happened to you happened for a reason.

'No,' he explained, 'I don't mean any of that rubbish about predestination, as if your whole life was planned out for you by something or someone and that you had no control over it. That way lies cowardice. Some things happen by accident, which really means it happens for reasons we don't understand because we don't have enough information. Other things happen because of someone else's actions and, if that's the case, it is clear for everyone to see. Otherwise, things happen because you do something yourself. In that case, the reward is yours, or if the results are bad, the blame is yours. Always accept the blame when something is your fault. Never blame what happens on someone else or something else — and that includes blaming God or the devil. If you did it, it's down to you. You and you alone. Always be honest. You might make mistakes. Everybody makes mistakes. But never deliberately blame someone or something else for what you are, in fact, responsible.'

Mr Best was most energetic during this little speech. Peter understood it completely and never forgot it. At least, not while he was with Mr Best. He came to think of Mr Best as a kind of second father.

Peter remembered all this as he looked at his statue. Statue seemed to be reminding him that it is *you* who make the everyday decisions. They are called everyday decisions because they are decisions that each of us makes every day of our lives. They may be small decisions; they may be big. They might involve money; they might involve honesty. But Statue was telling him, 'It isn't me, your statue, that tells you what is right or wrong; it is *you* and it always will be.'

Statue almost smiled as it seemed to say, 'Got it?'

Messing about with Boats

The following week, Peter, as per plan — for he always planned out his life — waited for the first fine day and went off to the boating lake in Peeshom Park which was an hour's cycle ride away from home. The boating lake was a fairly good size; good, that is, for sailing model boats of various kinds. There was no "proper" boating on the lake which was, in any case, not very deep, so that it was modellers who had the place to themselves. Peter didn't have a boat himself, unfortunately, for his parents didn't earn very much money and couldn't afford to buy him one. Peter understood the situation perfectly well and wasn't resentful but that didn't mean that he couldn't go and watch other people's boats. In any case, not all the modellers were children. Some of the larger, more ambitious boats — small ships really — were far too fancy and expensive for kids. There were several other children like Peter who had no model. Everyone seemed happy either watching or sailing the sailboats, the motor launches and even the miniature steamers. Some of the sailboats where simply set up, given a gentle push and left to the wind's devices. Others had radio-control of their sail settings and might be involved in races with similar boats during the day.

Peter particularly liked watching those. The launches and steamers had remote control of both direction and speed.

Although he would spend several happy hours watching the boats from vantage points near to the operators of these remote-controlled model boats, Peter often went for a stroll around the lake to watch how the boats fared when far away from their owners. On this day, while doing just that, Peter came upon another boy of about his own age who was trying to launch his boat well away from the pack. Peter reckoned that he was probably doing this for the first time and wanted some privacy while he messed up. And he did mess up, unfortunately, for his little yacht had sailed into some reeds growing in the water at this very muddy end of the lake.

The lad had what seemed to Peter to be a good remote controller, but it was clear that something had tangled up the rudder below watermark, and the boat was held fast. There was nothing to be done but to wade out and untangle the thing and that's what the boy had begun to do, having stripped off to his underwear and leaving the rest of his clothes on the bank of the lake. Unfortunately, there was more mud in this area than was obvious from the bank and in no time at all, the boy had sunk up to his chest in the stuff and couldn't move either forwards or back. He didn't seem to be in danger of drowning for the lake was fairly shallow everywhere — and, indeed, he was standing on the bottom — but he just couldn't move. He tried very hard at one point but, with his legs held fast, he just fell over. Now that *was* quite dangerous, of course, because he might have ended up with his head under water without any possibility of righting himself. That hadn't happened, fortunately, but Peter could see the danger.

At various points around the lake, there were emergency rescue stations, each being furnished with a lifebuoy. The nearest was not too far away and Peter took the lifebuoy ring and threw it out to the marooned boy, making sure to keep hold of the rope which was fortunately already attached to it. It's not usual for ropes to be already tied to lifebuoys but Peter had been lucky. Especially lucky because his first throw was wide of the mark and the boy couldn't reach it. Peter was able to haul the buoy in to shore again and try for a second time. That was much better. Indeed, the buoy — which had a relatively heavy, cork inner core — actually hit the boy on his head. It must have been quite painful.

Anyway, the lad grasped the buoy and Peter began to haul buoy and boy to shore. Nothing moved at first, so hard stuck in the mud was the lad, but with a heavy slurp and popping sound, he came free. However, it turned out that he could swim so, with his feet now well clear of the mud beneath, he swam the few metres further out and rescued his entangled boat from the reeds before turning back to shore. All was well and, while Peter put the lifebuoy back on its stand, the boy tried to clean himself up a bit before walking over to

Peter to thank him for saving his bacon. He introduced himself as Joel Munsterman.

It turned out that he went to the same school as Peter and was, in fact, in the same class. The reason why Peter hadn't seen him before was that Joel's family had moved into the area only a couple of weeks earlier. So, it was more accurate to say that Joel and Peter would be classmates next term, when school began again after the holiday. Peter and Joel became good friends over the next few holiday weeks and often came to Peeshom Park lake, to sail and watch the boats. As time went by, Peter began to see that Joel was not only a nice guy but a clever one too.

Exam Time

The next term heralded examinations: and pretty important ones they were. The term was planned out to be two weeks of new material and/or recapitulation of old, followed by extensive formal and informal revision right up to the examinations proper. Exam papers would be marked within the last two weeks of term and important decisions would be made as to which stream each student would go to from then on. So, these were very important examinations for all students as their results could determine how the rest of their studies went; and, ultimately, how the rest of their lives might go.

Peter was a passably good student. Not in the top drawer; he knew that. But good enough, he hoped, to make it through to the A stream and so onwards and upwards. He had been working very hard for these exams already for he understood their importance completely. He reckoned that some boys in class didn't really see how important they were but that was their problem, of course.

Peter's determination came from his observing his dad. His father didn't have a very good job, it didn't pay much, and he clearly didn't like it. Peter was perceptive enough to see what grit his dad showed, however, because he never — or almost never — complained and always did his best to look after Peter and his mother. So, while he loved his father and admired his character, Peter was determined to do better in life. He wanted a good education such as his dad, through no fault of his own (for in those days almost all pupils left school by the time they reached thirteen), had not received and so get the best chance of a good, worthwhile job in due course. When Mr Best had asked Peter what sort of job he wanted, however, he had been unable to say. He just did not know enough about jobs at this stage.

'Don't worry about that,' Mr Best had said. 'There's plenty of time to find out. Just keep on with your schoolwork.' Mr Best really was like a second father.

Exam time came around very quickly. Peter found the first two papers quite easy; anyway, he had managed to answer all the questions and thought that he had made a good stab at the answers. Then came the weekend before they would begin again. He wasn't looking forward to the next exam paper for it was history, a subject he was not particularly fond of; nor the one after that which was to be literature. Peter liked reading but he'd found the set books rather boring and he hadn't understood what they were really about. So, he spent a restless Saturday worrying about Tuesday's exams.

Monday was a day free of exams and students in his class were free to stay at home revising or resting if they wanted, or to spend time at school. As long as they were quiet — because other classes were taking exams on Monday — they were free to come and go. Peter decided to go to school on Monday. At one point, he was wandering about near his form room which was empty. Peter went in and closed the door and went to his desk. He thought he might find some inspiration on history or literature from his textbooks there. He sat down and opened one and began to read but it was no good. He was saturated from all the revision he had done in his other subjects and he just couldn't buckle down to reading subjects he disliked.

It was then that he made the fateful decision. He knew that exam papers were locked in the steel cupboard next to the master's desk. Peter always carried those skeleton keys he'd bought from his favourite junk shop so long ago. He went up to the metal cupboard and tried to pick the lock. It was a simple lock, far easier than those he had practised on before. He had the cupboard open in no time. He pushed the cupboard door closed and went to the classroom door, quietly opened it and looked about. There was nobody around. There was no sound of anyone. He went back into the room, closed the door, and returned to the cupboard. He found several envelopes marked "Examination". The trouble was, though, that they were all sealed, and Peter had no equipment with him to unseal them without leaving a trace. He could have given it up then and there. He knew he could. He knew he should. But he didn't. He kept looking through the packets, but they were all sealed. Then, right at the back of the cupboard, away from the pile of exam envelopes, he saw one separate package all on its own. He read the inscription: "Master Copies".

And it wasn't sealed!

Peter took it out of the cupboard, carefully removed the sheets of paper inside and, in almost no time at all, he found two sheets stapled together and headed "History". A little deeper in the pile, he discovered "Literature". Peter found an empty envelope of the same size in the cupboard and slipped the two exam papers inside. He made sure everything else in the cupboard was exactly as it had been when he first opened the door. He was sure. He closed the door and, using his skeleton keys once more, locked it. His heart was beating fit to bust as he opened the classroom door, checked again that nobody was around and, as casually as he could, strolled along the corridor with his envelope under his arm. He went next into the school library where he knew there was a small photocopier. Again, he was lucky. Nobody was near and nobody came in as he hurriedly copied the two sets of exam papers. He quickly — but without running even though he sorely wanted to — returned to his form-room and unlocked the metal cupboard again. He replaced the originals of the history and literature examination papers — and he knew they were the originals rather than the copies because they were stapled together — relocked the cupboard door and left the classroom one more time. In all that time, he had neither seen nor heard anyone. Of course, the rest of the school were either at home or in examinations; even so, he had been lucky. Peter left the school and hurried back to his room at home.

He was so excited, so pleased with his daring robbery that he told Statue what he had done. Statue was stony-faced. Well, he was made of stone, after all. Peter only saw a blank expression on Statue's face at first but, as he calmed down and stopped breathing so heavily, he thought he saw a look of disappointment creep into Statue's expression.

'Well, look here, Statue,' Peter said, 'it is ever so important that I pass all my exams this year and I really am useless at history and literature. I won't be doing anybody else out of a place but I might just get myself into the A class next year. I so much want Mum and Dad to be proud of me.'

Then he thought: *They wouldn't be proud if they knew I'd cheated.* He thought he saw Statue's expression soften at that thought.

'How can you read my thoughts, Statue?' Peter said but it seemed it had.

Well, regardless, Peter took out the exam papers and began to read them. He discovered that, together with the typed questions were hand-written answers. He had struck gold! Although Peter was pretty awful at these subjects, he did have a good memory and it did not take him too long to remember enough questions together with their answers for him to pass with a good mark. He worked pretty hard at all this cribbing until his mother called him down for tea.

'Have you been revising?' she asked.

After tea, Peter went out for a walk. He began by rehearsing the questions and answers of tomorrow's exams but, after a while he became saturated and just had to stop doing that. Then he tried to think of nothing at all but found that quite impossible. He kept thinking of how Statue had looked at him. He kept thinking of what Mr Best would say if he knew what he'd done. But then he thought, *I can't undo what I've done even if I wanted to. I must keep going now.*

He didn't look at Statue when he got home to his room. He went straight to bed and, surprisingly perhaps, he fell into a deep sleep straight away. He was exhausted.

Next day, Peter arrived at school in good time for the start of the first examination. The thought suddenly occurred to him: *Suppose the "Master Exam" papers he'd found were only a first draft? Suppose the exam paper he was about to turn over and read was a second or third draft and bore little resemblance to the original?*

He felt quite panicky and didn't exactly know whether he hoped that such would be the case or not.

'Turn over your papers,' called out the invigilating teacher. The paper before him was *exactly* like that he had taken from the cupboard; *exactly* like the one he had (mostly) memorised. Peter wrote rapidly, trying to remember the answers he had read but, at the same time, changing the wording a bit so that he wouldn't give himself away. He was also careful not to finish all the necessary questions and to keep on scratching right to the time when he heard the customary, 'Stop writing now.' It all seemed to have gone well. Peter reckoned that he would get a good mark on that paper. He went off for his lunch feeling rather smug.

Something similar happened with the literature paper in the afternoon. Again, there were no surprises and he went home with a sense of having got his two worst subjects off his back. When he got back to his room, he laughed and said to Statue, 'Well, I guess I did the right thing. I should make it into the A stream now.'

He glanced at the bust. It seemed to be scowling at him. And, while before its colour was a uniform yellow-brown he thought that now he detected a darker brown streak running across the chest into the armpit on the left side.

Odd, Peter thought, *I haven't seen that before; I don't think so, anyway.*

At teatime, his mother asked him how the exams had gone that day and Peter answered that everything seemed tickety-boo. His mum seemed so pleased. Peter didn't revise any more for the following day's exam — he felt happy enough about it — and stayed downstairs for a while to watch television with his parents. That was a bit unusual, his mother thought.

Accusations

As usual, the teachers had worked very hard and marked all the papers within one week of the end of the last examination. And, as planned in great detail by the examinations officer — who was actually Peter's mathematics teacher — results were posted on the main school notice board at ten a.m. precisely on the following Monday morning. All the students gathered round the notice board to see how well they had done. Students were listed in order of total marks gained. Peter, at number eighteen, had passed in all his subjects, including history and literature, and had distinguished himself in chemistry and physics. Other students had done a lot better than that, but Peter was happy enough. He knew he had done well enough to enter the A stream next year. Mission accomplished!

As is usual on these occasions, once he had satisfied himself about his own results, Peter looked at those of some of his classmates. By and large, he thought everyone had done as well as expected. The top ten names were exactly as one might have forecast and… wait a moment, there was Joel Munsterman at number two in the list. Peter had long known that his friend was a clever fellow, but he hadn't realised that he was that clever.

That's good, thought Peter, for he wasn't a mean-spirited chap, and after all, he had long realised that his boating friend was rather sharp. So, all in all, everything had turned out well and most students were pleased with what they had achieved. Mind you, it was a shame about Knowlesie who had missed out on the A stream. Peter knew him quite well and saw how hard he had worked for these exams. Denis Knowles was visibly upset with his results. The problem is that only so many students made it into the A stream. There was a cut-off point and he'd just missed out.

Peter explained to Statue that it was unlikely that his cheating would have made any difference to Knowlesie because, 'I would have made the cut anyway.' Statue stared stonily. 'Then why did I cheat?' Peter asked himself. Exactly. Statue seemed to agree. 'Well, it's done,' Peter concluded. 'The exams are over so let's get on with life.' He didn't feel too sure about it though.

Early in the last week of term, a thunderbolt hit the class. It turned out that Joel Munsterman's answers for his literature paper were virtually perfect; just too good to be true. And, by accident really, the form teacher had discovered that someone had interfered with his examination master scripts.

How on earth was he able to do that? wondered Peter, with considerable anguish. Joel was accused of cheating. He protested for all he was worth, but the form master and headmaster were both adamant and disgusted. Joel was to be expelled from the school immediately. There was, of course, an enormous kerfuffle with Joel's father visiting the headmaster. Students heard a blistering row going on in the head's study even behind the closed door, but Joel's expulsion was confirmed. Peter saw Joel in the corridor at one point. He was in tears and was insisting to one of his teachers that he was innocent, that he was certainly not a cheat. The teacher was obviously sympathetic but could do nothing. In due course, a formal notice of the expulsion was pinned on the main school notice board in the assembly hall. Everybody knew that Joel Munsterman was a cheat. Everyone except Peter and Joel himself.

Peter felt awful. He was so sorry. He was sorry for Joel. He was sorry for Joel's family who had just moved into the area and might now have to move away. But above all, Peter was sorry for himself. He paced up and down in his room asking himself over and over why it was him that had had that temptation. If he had no skeleton keys, he wouldn't have been able to open the cupboard door. If there had been some people around in the school that day, he wouldn't have been able to get away with the theft. He wouldn't have been able to go to the library and copy the exam papers. If he hadn't needed to prove himself to his father by making sure of getting into the A stream…

'Why me?' he wailed.

He glanced at the bust. Statue's expression was thunderous. Peter had never seen it look so black. That dark stain across its chest had turned into some sort of fissure. It was as if Statue was broken. Peter ran out of his room, out of the house, and kept running until he was exhausted.

After some time, he slowly began to walk back home. He walked as if he were broken himself. He was so miserable. He didn't think about what Joel must be feeling, though. Peter went back to his room and threw himself on his bed. When his mother called him down for tea, he went but ate very little.

'What's the matter, Peter?' she asked but he could only mumble and went back to his room.

'Why did this happen to me?' he asked again and lay down on his bed once more. After a long time, he thought, *I just can't go to the headmaster and admit to what I've done. I shall just have to live with it, keep quiet forevermore about it. I shall not think about it again.*

Peter looked across at Statue. Before his eyes, the brown fissure across its chest opened and the statue began to part into two pieces.

'I wish I'd never clapped eyes on you,' Peter said out loud.

Statue slowly began to crumble. Before Peter's gaze, the sandstone bust slowly became just a formless pile of sand. Peter was devastated. All he could think of were Mr Best's words: 'You must take responsibility for your own actions. Stop looking for scapegoats. It is *you* who must decide. *You* who must act.'

Reality and Conscience

Peter never got over that business. In the years that followed, he felt guilty all the time and couldn't stop thinking about it. If anything went wrong in his life, he always felt that it was because of his actions back then. In one sense, he had learned his lesson well. He did indeed understand that he must turn to himself — to his conscience — for guidance in all things. There was nothing wrong in asking other people for advice, but decisions were his alone. Joel had changed school, had managed to swallow the injustice done to him, and had gone on to make a fine school and university record for himself. He was working in an interesting job, one he really wanted, and was happy. He had put his past behind him. But, sad to say, Peter was a broken man. It was likely that he would be in torment forever.

Anyway, years later, well after he had left school and was earning his living for himself, Peter suddenly got the urge to trace Statue's maker, the sculptor, Mrs Heatherington. He remembered that she lived in Linghelm Place. He didn't know which house, but he reckoned that all he had to do was to ask at the first one he came to and eventually he was bound to trace her. And he was right for, after only the third attempt he got directions. He walked up to the lady's front door, knocked, and when it opened, asked if Mrs Heatherington lived there. She was getting on by now though was by no means old or decrepit. She invited Peter in and asked what she could do for him.

Peter explained how, years ago, he had bought a sandstone bust within a glazed frame from the junk shop in the high street and that he had been told that she had been the sculptor.

Mrs Heatherington looked at Peter in astonishment for some moments and said, 'No, I didn't make the sculpture you describe. I've never made a sculpture in my life. I'm not a sculptor. I wouldn't know where to begin.'

It was Peter's turn to be surprised but he thanked her and apologised for troubling her.

It occurred to him that the junk shop trader might have made a mistake. What was his name? Ah, yes; Raymond. Peter resolved to check with him — if he was still there, of course, and Peter was far from sure about that. But he was. Older but with his renowned acute memory.

Yes, he remembered Peter. 'That young lad who came in from time to time.'

'Do you remember my buying a statue from you? I paid half a quid for it,' Peter asked.

'I do remember your buying a funny bent screwdriver once. Oh, yes! And a joke book and a set of skeleton keys. Did you ever manage to make them work, by the way?'

'What about the statue?' Peter asked him urgently.

'No, I don't remember a statue,' Raymond replied, 'and I have always had a marvellous memory. I know everything that passed through my shop. I know that's crazy, but I do. Describe this statue.'

Peter gave him a detailed description — sandstone, framed and glazed; every detail.

'Well, obviously you have a clear memory of it, but I don't remember it at all. Whereabouts in the shop did you find it?' he continued.

He was obviously trying to be helpful for he remembered Peter as a young lad perfectly well.

'It was behind the front door, half-hidden by your coat hanging from a hook on the wall,' Peter replied.

'I've never hung my coat from a hook behind the door,' the shopkeeper replied, 'Nor has anyone else. Look, there isn't a hook there. There never has been. There's no place to put one because the panelling there isn't strong enough to support any weight.'

Peter gave up. Had he just imagined it all? Had Statue ever actually existed? Had he just been talking to his conscience all those months when he was a young boy?

…and now for something altogether
lighter:

ROMP

Groan

What a really beautiful morning! A sparkling blue sky graced with but a few wispy clouds, mostly white, although some even grey, brushed along by a gentle wind which is the last remains of that stormy night with its heavy showers. That rain has left a cool nip in this new-born morning's air. That rain has cracked the delicate perfume vial of the opening of the day. That rain has washed away yesterday's dust to gift this morning such clarity that you can almost count each leaf on the trees covering those distant hills.

The camelia buds are about to burst open. 'Look at us!' they preen. 'Are we not beautiful?'

The morning is quieter than usual as if the birds themselves are in awe of this grand opening. It's true. Listen! No raucous calls. Hardly a chirrup breaks the silence. Listen harder, though. What do you hear? Nothing? Listen very carefully. Concentrate now and you will begin to catch that ever-so-gentle straining sound. It's very quiet indeed but there it is… A group-heaving, swelling across the garden. It always happens after night rain, that soft crescendo, that growing assertion, that groan as thousands upon thousands, no! millions upon millions, of weeds thrust their way up through the softened soil. Into *your* garden! What are they saying, those tasteless intruders into your precious domestic tidiness? Why, they are stretching of course, they're taking a deep breath, they are proclaiming the wonder of just being alive.

'*Allons, enfants,* come, comrades, let us grow together onwards and upwards. This is our chance. Hurry! Be strong! Let us cover the earth.'

They probably mean just the earth in and around your flower beds but judging by their enthusiasm, maybe they mean the Earth itself.

'Damn it,' you say, 'I was really looking forward to a restful weekend. All I wanted was to sit in my favourite chair, to read my paper and to drink my coffee. Is that too much to hope for? I can accept not winning the lottery, but my weekend laze is surely sacrosanct.'

Groan, heave, swell, grow…

So it is that, with moaning and groaning of your own (well, if they can groan, why can't you?), you change into your "dirties", collect a trowel and bucket from the back of the garage, and kneel down in front of the first clumps of green shoots. The weeds probably think it appropriate that you kneel before them. After all, they have the power to move you; to move you out of your chair and away from your weekend paper. But no! You kneel because your back will give you hell later if you bend from the waist. You begin to pull. It's fortunate that the weeds are new for they haven't grown strong anchors yet. Out they come! But you mustn't be careless and just grab handfuls of them, so many there are, or you will break some stems and leave the roots in the ground and then, as soon as you turn your back, they'll return all the stronger for their ordeal. It's going to be a long, long, slow job but you must be disciplined about it. Careful now! Don't pull that one, that's a young freesia shoot. So difficult to tell the difference at this stage. It could have been grass, couldn't it? Just pull the weeds.

What's the difference between a flower and a weed? It is cutely claimed that a weed is a flower in the wrong place. Those weeds in amongst the grasses in yonder meadow all help to firm up cover, to maintain and encourage biodiversity, maybe to provide a little colour in amongst the green grass. But your garden is *not* a meadow. It is an outdoor painting which you have painstakingly built, constructed, lovingly grown, over many years and at considerable cost.

'So, weeds: you are growing in the wrong place.'

'That's not fair. That's discrimination. We have rights. You are the sort of being that likes butterflies but hates moths. Why?'

'Because butterflies are beautiful and moths are plain and because moths tend to fly and flutter at and around me in large numbers while butterflies rarely gather in groups of more than two... and anyway, they're so delicate and sweet.'

'So deferential, you mean. They know their place.'

'Well, now you mention it, they do add to the order and delicacy of my garden. They bring twinkle to the scene. They seem to give approval to my gardening efforts.'

'But it's not about you and your pernickety rearrangements of Nature's splendour. All creatures are adapted to their environment. We weeds are superbly well adapted. We can cover the whole of your garden in hours.'

'Overrun, you mean.'

'One man's overrun is another's triumphal great march. Beauty is in the eye of the beholder.'

'Like taste, of course. The flowers and other plants which I and other gardeners choose to put into our gardens are so much more refined than weeds. Most weeds grow fast and spread, either on top of the ground or under it. Their purpose in life is merely to grow, to reproduce and to smother. Those with flowers only produce tiny affairs which are insignificant and coarse. *Proper* flowers, on the other hand, grow much more slowly or, if not, in a strictly disciplined way and they seem to put their energies into making beautiful leaves and flowers. They have taste, you know, not just brute strength.'

'My, my, what a snob you are! What an awful example of discrimination.'

'There's nothing wrong with discrimination. The whole point of experience in life, of education, is to learn enough to make deliberate and defensible discriminations — choices — rather than simply to follow whatever comes up next. I have absolutely no intention of apologising for discriminating.'

'That's telling them!'

'Who's that?'

'I am one of your prized and cared-for flowers and let me tell you I much prefer to put my energies into growing into a nice shape and producing beautiful flowers for the butterflies and bees to enjoy than to defend myself from greedy weeds. So, let me tell you now: I support the gardener every time. He has my vote!'

'Why, how nice of you to say so. I shall pay especial attention to you in my rounds.'

'How cosy!' sneers a weed. 'Let me tell you that there are more of us. We will bury you. You can't have gardeners around for ever and everywhere and, without their interference, you will be lost. Strength in numbers, that's what it is.'

'That's rule by force!' a cyclamen complained, 'There's no justice in that. It would be a sad world if only the strong were to survive. Grey, boring, unimaginative, sad.'

'No! It would be a glorious world where the strong come together and form a dominion of power without the possibility of snobbish, prissy creatures imposing their minority will upon we rightful rulers, all in the name of education, learning, expertise and knowledge.'

'Well I've heard enough. I'm the gardener around here and I can see the strength of the weeds' argument. Power rules — always. I shall now exercise that power and pull up all offending plants which I deem to be ugly and/or in the wrong place. Don't feel too badly about it, weeds. You have a purpose. You will make marvellous compost.'

That told 'em.

The Boss

My wife and I are frequently pestered by a couple of currawongs. We have been feeding these birds regularly for a few years now so we can hardly complain. That isn't to say that we don't complain, of course, for we have long believed that consistency in one's views, though holy, merely presages dullness. Our complaint is that, by now, these two birds should know full well that mealtimes are early morning and mid/late afternoon. We don't do lunches. Our feathered friends have obviously heard about hope springing eternal, that lightning may strike anywhere at any time, and that I continue to buy lottery tickets. From right across the garden, they notice the moment I begin moving around in the kitchen, pricking the spuds ready for baking or composing a slow-cooked casserole, either of which tasks might be begun some considerable time before our mealtime, let alone theirs. One or both of them swoop in and perch on the narrow ledge outside our wide kitchen window. Their accusatory stares and their beak-knocking on the windowpane both eventually take their toll on my assumed blindness. Mind you, I'm no pushover. I wait till half an hour at least before their "regular" teatime before giving in.

I prepare — if that's the right word — their tea of bread and grapes (they cost me a fortune in grapes, by the way, and I feel guilty if I take even just a few for myself at lunch) and then open an adjacent door onto the deck where I set down my twice-daily offerings. One of the birds immediately hops down from its perch on the window ledge and begins to eat; it always begins with a grape. The other bird flies off to perch on a branch of a fig tree just a couple of metres away.

'For you!' I say to the bird trying to manipulate an over-sized grape in its gaping maw, and in a louder voice directed at the bird in the tree, 'And for you, scaredy-cat.'

I retreat inside and close the door. After a moment or two, the first-mentioned bird flies off and the other leaves its tree perch and samples the meal, taking a piece or two of bread. By the way, the bird which does most of the pestering on the window ledge is the one which eventually retreats to the fig tree.

I have presented you with this quotidian scene in order to ask what seems to me to be an interesting question. Which is the male bird and which the female? I make the assumption that there's one of each for they always go around together, never shoo one another off from the grub, and generally seem to get along swimmingly (or should that be flappingly?). Of course, they could be gay; but let's not complicate matters. Allow me to elaborate the question a little. Is it the female who, when I open the door, backs off and perches in the tree so as to let her man take first dibs because, being female, she knows her place? Or is it the male who flies off into the tree so as to show due courtesy to his mate? Or should I rephrase these two possibilities in order to protect myself from the outraged sensibilities of my distaff? I'm sure the question is answerable simply by recourse to the notion of the dominance of the male in order to protect his mate. Am I correct in assuming that only humans have the notion of gentlemanliness? Then again, what if it's the females who do the aggression bit. I tried half-heartedly to find out via our good friend, Google, but was inevitably led into well-established studies of chickens which is all well and good if you want to know who "Madam" is within a group of females. I leave it to my reader to research further as I'm more interested here in the question than in the answer. May I opine that such a stance often suggests itself in our busy lives?

However, if you cannot resist forming an opinion on these vexing questions, may I remind you of what came before all this? You know: all that stuff about respect for education. I really must insist that truth and evidence are sadly all too rare these days. It would be unfair to blame Twitter and all the other forms of modern, digital intercourse but they certainly don't help. They do bear some responsibility for the fact that one doubts — or conversely, instantly and firmly believes, as the case may be — just about everything in print. Once upon a time, as they quaintly used to say, what you saw in print, at least the material in serious-looking media, could be relied upon. Or could it? Maybe we were simply used to according respect for others' work automatically. Maybe it was always true that any and all opinions should be checked. Then, of course, we come to the question of how we might do that checking. If we can perform a simple experiment, we can be convinced or otherwise in a moment, but most assertions do not yield readily to experimental verification. What then? We might consult an encyclopaedia or other learned tome; preferably several. Today, we might consult Wikipedia. We might, but there is no guarantee that all entries in that remarkable source are free of error. Here and there, Wikipedia itself draws its readers' attention to that fact. Sometimes, Wikipedia includes data and opinions from other sources which are themselves in error. There's an awful lot to this checking business and it undoubtedly helps to consult other people for they, in turn, may have consulted many sources of their own.

Of course, most of us are just too busy to spend the time necessary to educate ourselves properly about every last thing so we need sources which experience, and reputation, lead us to trust. Trust. Surely, that is what is being eroded, accidentally and deliberately, by so many modern media. And I intend the word *media*, plural of medium, to refer to just about any means of disseminating information, news, opinion, humour or advertising.

Neighbours

My neighbour, Ed Hershowitz, looked over our shared garden fence the other day, while I was closely inspecting the progress of some canna lily bulbs I had planted, several weeks earlier. I inspect them every day.

'You won't make them grow any faster by staring at them,' he said.

'Mind your own business!' I replied. (We always pretend annoyance at one another.) 'You don't know what you're talking about. How on earth do you think these plants will know which way is up without my telling them regularly?'

Ed shares my views about weeds, by the way. Indeed, we share many notions in common, but especially about gardening and of how we make homes of our houses. I don't agree with him, however, on his choice of the colour of his front door. Most front doors in this neighbourhood are black or white or natural wood. That's the sort of thing preferred by most folk around these parts. I have, on occasion, teased Ed about his doubtful taste.

'For God's sake: purple! Ed, must you be so obnoxious? Toe the line, do!'

As my dear, long-gone dad used to say: "His taste is in his mouth."

Ed growls at me to mind my own goddam business but there's a twinkle in his eye. 'Just keep reading the newspapers,' he replies.

We laugh and maybe I should tell you why. The thing is, you see, that Ed's neighbour on the other side, a Mrs Seeall Bounty, shares my view about Ed's affront but she takes it all far, far too much to heart. On more than one occasion, she has telephoned him at work, carefully choosing times when she knew full well that he wasn't actually at work. She knew that, by the way, because she could see him sitting on a deckchair in his back garden reading, she assumed, a novel or something salacious, maybe. As a matter of fact, Ed was doing some background reading in relation to his work. I have told him that he should attach a large note to his deckchair announcing the subject of his reading matter so that Mrs Bounty might be properly informed. Anyway, the reason why she chooses to ring him at work while he is at home is in order to leave a message for him with his associates.

'Well,' she exclaims with great indignation, 'I have called several times and it seems that he is never in his workplace. It is disgraceful (she emphasises the "g", by the way). I shall write to a national newspaper.'

I don't know for sure, of course, but I visualise her as slamming down the phone. Or whatever passes for that in these days of the mobile.

Ed's work colleagues pass on Mrs Bounty's messages with some degree of glee and go back to their proper duties. Ed laps it all up and keeps me posted on each round.

'You see, Sam: you're not the only one who hates me,' he says, and his features assume a configuration I can only describe as a pout.

'But a *national* newspaper!' I exclaim. 'You will become famous. Our whole neighbourhood will become famous.'

'Yeah,' he replies, 'like Rillington Place.'

'Or Peyton Place, maybe?' I suggest.

We become increasingly enthusiastic with it all as Ed and I muse about headlines in the National Wailer about *The Weed Murderers of Rillington Place* or concerning *The Man who Kisses his Wife every Tuesday Evening in Full View of the Neighbours.*

The trouble is that this notion of writing to a national newspaper has taken on with us a life of its own. Whenever something occurs in the world or even in our own backyard which gives us cause for concern, we immediately assert that we will write to a national newspaper. And all because Ed chose to paint his front door purple.

Ed does not, I'm sorry to say, enjoy perfect health. He has some cancer or other which will, in time, kill him off. He knows this full well and has accepted the idea of a guillotine poised and at the ready hanging over his neck. He sees his oncologist every three months after a new CT scan — which is a sort of three-dimensional X-ray, by the way — for his analysis and recommendations. He has been in remission, meaning on hold, in hiatus or so-far-so-good for a long time now. Ed regularly tells this specialist that he intends to hang around on this earth for another twenty years, *at least,* and he always emphasises that last bit. Both Ed and his doctor know full well that his fate lies in the lap of the gods, but Ed cannot help but add — and he says it every time he attends an assessment: 'And it's *your* job to see that I do!'

Ed insists that without humour, life is empty. I must say I agree completely. Anyway, the last time Ed presented himself for another consultation with the great man was during the time of the dreaded Covid pandemic. There were no magazines scattered around the doctor's waiting room because, of course, they were deemed a likely medium for spreading the disease. Ed was well aware of the reason for the absence of reading material in the room but could not let the occasion go to waste. When his oncologist came out of his room to greet him and his wife, who was in on the act that day, Ed complained loudly to his doctor — loudly enough for the doctor's receptionist to hear:

'It really is not good enough to remove your customary literature from the waiting room. I have missed out on my usual scoop of new, old recipes. I shall withdraw my custom.' He paused before adding, 'I shall write to a national newspaper!'

Ed's wife, who's heard it all before, turned to the receptionist to help calm the situation. 'Bless. He doesn't get out much, you know.'

Ed and his dear lady-wife are acquiring quite a reputation in those premises. I think the doctor and his receptionist look forward to his visits; although I do wonder what they would think of his purple front door.

Some new people recently moved into a house a few doors away. They clearly have an awful lot of money for they have had builders in, changing just about everything in the place. That's all right, of course; it's their place after all and they can do what they want with it. But it's also okay for the rest of us to look at what they're doing and take a view. It's natural after all to be nosey. You can't help it, can you? The thing is, these new folk, are such show-offs. They have totally ignored the well-established style of the house they purchased — and of all the houses immediately around it — by making extensions and modifications as if they're building a Californian Trivago hotel or something. Ed and I refer to the place as Trivago House. I mean, if you want to live in an hotel, go to an hotel. Several other neighbours and near-neighbours dismiss the new people as *Nouveau Riche*, meaning New Money, in an attempt to sneer at those whose wealth has been acquired only within their own lifetimes, with the implication that it takes a long time, even generations, to understand the subtlety, culture and taste of Old Money acquired a long time ago. The sneer is, of course, just another example of ultimate snobbery. Sure: there are people who are totally lacking in taste — but, of course, who is to decide? — and there is no guarantee that the amassed loot of several generations will save any given person from that fate. The best you can do, I suppose, is to select friends with similar tastes to your own.

Anyway, I raised this matter really only to acquaint you with my mate, Ed's, take on the *Nouveau Riche*. He calls them *New Richards*, so taking a swipe at one's linguistic pretentions as well.

Ed rather likes taking swipes at people who he sees as being pretentious. Maybe he's over-sensitive to other folks' foibles but I do rather like the way he summarises a most highly qualified academic chap of our acquaintance who, in Ed's opinion, lacks down-to-earth common sense; not an uncommon pairing, I must say.

'More degrees than a thermometer,' chuckles Ed, 'but can't get to the point of anything, no matter how long he takes.'

'You'd better not say that to his face, Ed,' I replied one day.

'Why not?' he said. 'It's a free country. I am entittled.'

'You mean "entitled" I do believe,' I chastised.

'Yes, that's right; entittled,' he replied. When Ed has a bee in his bonnet, nothing will shift it. He will speak the language as he likes. He is entittled.

Aim High

It's been a busy, busy day. I'm getting a bit tired and I'm making the odd mistake while cooking our evening meal.

'I'm trying my best,' I wail.

'You *do* do best,' replies my ever-sympathetic wife and moves towards the fridge and a cold bottle as it's now wine o'clock.

It's nice to be comforted. And, of course, I could always go out and buy a takeaway meal from any number of places. That would cost more and I'm tight. Much more to the point, though, is that takeaways never taste as good as home-cooking: well, not in our house. I grant that I can't compete with the cooking you get in a proper flash restaurant and I do enjoy going to one of those occasionally. Indeed, we'll go again just as soon as I can arrange for a second mortgage. However, even simple fare can taste wonderful provided it's made carefully. Pay attention; try; think about what you like in a posh restaurant and try to work out why you like it. Read lots of recipes. You will soon learn which writers provide sensible instruction, which like the food themselves; indeed, which probably actually use their recipes and criticise their own creations. They *are* out there.

'Why bother?' you say? Well, because nothing in this world comes out right without effort or, at least, not reliably so. You might succeed by accident but just you wait until you try the same meal out on your favourite guests.

'It worked last time.' So it did, old sport, but you've made a right hash of it this time. Time to dash out for a take-away? At least, those guys are pretty consistent. The same old cardboard every time but you can, at least, depend on it.

SmartBell

I must return to that front door: Ed has been on the lookout for a new doorbell for some time. He's unimpressed with what he sees as the same old boring chimes, cuckoo calls, or even good old plain rings. He wants to control the outcome of any visitor pushing on his bell. He argues, with some validity I admit, that in these hyper-technical times, it should be possible to arrange that the bell push activates a recording of anything preordained by the houseowner. However, he's not been successful in his search for the necessary technical gismo. Instead, he has been doing a bit of homework in order to construct what he wants himself. So far, he has been able to arrange that a push on his front doorbell initiates a recording of a preprepared message left on his computer to be played through a loudspeaker sited immediately above the bell-pusher's head. Ed was even clever enough to avoid traipsing wiring all over the house, instead arranging for communication from bell to computer to loudspeaker to take place via wi-fi. I must say, Ed's a bright chap. I'm full of admiration. In the beginning, his message to all visitors was "Welcome to our humble abode; please state your name and business". However, the really smart part of Ed's setup is that he can change the message at any time by choosing from a group of messages left on his computer. Then he added to his toy by putting a sensor in his front door so that the house, so to speak, knows something about the visitor immediately, even before the bellpush is pushed.

Thus, in the middle of the front door is one of those small peep-hole thingies. You know, the sort of device you find in most hotel bedroom doors through which a guest can see who is standing outside while denying the visitor any view of the inside of the room. However, Ed has gone one better because the peephole is actually a miniature camera connected, once again, to his computer by wi-fi. Better still, everything which goes to his computer, also goes to his smartphone so Ed can see and hear his visitors from anywhere in his house; or, for that matter, from anywhere at all.

While all this might seem quite fun, there is a downside, of course, because, mindful of unwanted advertisements popping up in your computer mailbox, you might not want to be interrupted by visitors, all and sundry, when you are quietly having a snooze, reading the paper, cooking or sitting on the loo. Now Ed was quite a dab hand at computer programming in earlier days, so he decided to exploit his erstwhile skills and delegate the role of primary decider on what to do about any given visitor to his computer.

His first task at this point was to upload pictures of every regular visitor to his computer and to build into his computer program a face-recognition facility. Then, assigned to each of these listed visitors was some appropriate action. For example, when Maria, who is always welcome, walks up to the front door then, even before she manages to push the doorbell, his computer program has recognised her image from the door peephole, unlatches the door and plays a pre-recorded message saying, "Come in, Maria. Good to see you. We're in the kitchen. Come through". Actually, Ed's program is even smarter because the location — kitchen, for example — can be changed as appropriate to lounge or study, maybe, depending on where Ed's smartphone locates him. I did point out to him that he mightn't want to invite Maria or whoever to join him in the bathroom but good old Ed had thought of that and programmed his computer to say, "I'll meet you in the lounge in a moment" if he were indisposed in that way.

Every time I meet up with Ed, we have discussed the progress on his automatic welcoming system. He's been at it now for months and is enjoying himself hugely. He has included an option for recognised guests who may not be close enough friends for him to open the door to on every occasion or, indeed, for recognised guests to whom entry would never be granted. In either of these two cases, although his program recognises the guest as he or she walks up to the door, no message is broadcast until they actually ring the bell. Then the message might be, "Sorry but we are unavailable right now. Please call again. By the way, what can we help you with?" There are variations in which one or more of these short sentences are omitted depending on whether Ed wants to be polite, impolite, curt or downright awkward. He never gives the message "Sorry, we're out" for that advertises an empty house. And that might even be true! His automatic system also has the feature of telling a visitor to get lost: "… please don't call again". He was tempted to use lurid language but thought better of it. That could be fun but I think he's right. Above all, his system allows him to interrupt a standard message or to forestall it by speaking into his smartphone.

Ed has always recognised that computer programs cannot handle every possibility but that doesn't stop him endlessly trying to improve his automatic system. He's even arranged that the voice message given to regular, welcome, visitors can be varied in a pseudo-random way. "Come in, Maria. Good to see you. Nice hairdo. We're in the kitchen. Come through". He recognises that this could go badly wrong but reckons that good friends will tolerate errors in a spirit of fun.

I do so like Ed. He brings such colour to our world. Even if it is sometimes purple. His smart-bell has become quite sophisticated these days, by the way. It seems that it can recognise political pollsters a mile off.

'Go away! If you persist in pestering me — or even if you pesist pistering me — I shall write to a national newspaper!' it says and temporarily deactivates the bell.

'You can't do that, Ed!' I said when he demonstrated this latest facility.

'Why not?' he replied. 'It's my house. It's a free country. I am entittled!'